AWFUL
AARDVARK

Other books illustrated by Adrienne Kennaway:

Greedy Zebra
Hot Hippo
Crafty Chameleon
Tricky Tortoise
Lend Me Your Wings

Text copyright © 1989 by Peter Upton
Illustrations copyright © 1989 by Adrienne Kennaway

First U.S. edition

First published in Great Britain in 1989 by
Hodder and Stoughton Children's Books
a division of Hodder and Stoughton Ltd.
Mill Road, Dunton Green, Sevenoaks, Kent TN13 2YJ

Library of Congress Catalog Card Number 89-80028

10 9 8 7 6 5 4 3 2 1

Printed in Belgium

AWFUL AARDVARK

Mwalimu and
Adrienne Kennaway

Little, Brown and Company
Boston Toronto London

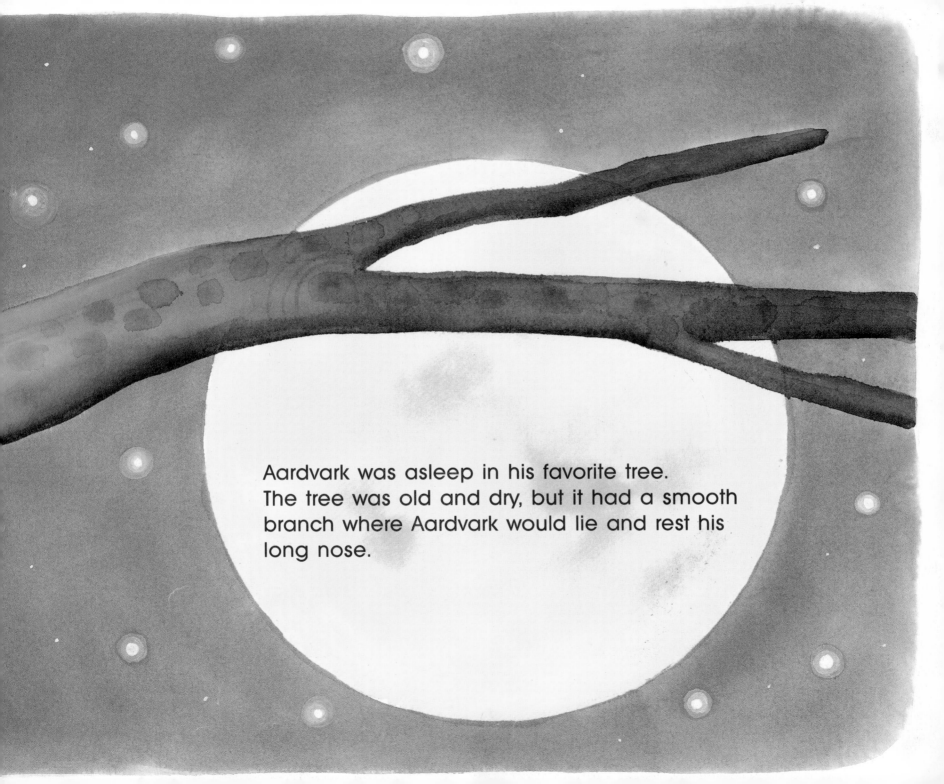

Aardvark was asleep in his favorite tree.
The tree was old and dry, but it had a smooth
branch where Aardvark would lie and rest his
long nose.

And what a nose!
His snoring was so loud
that it kept Mongoose
and all the other animals
awake night after night.
HHHRRR—ZZZZ!
went Aardvark's nose.
  "How awful,"
Mongoose yawned.
"I wish he would
keep quiet or go
somewhere else."

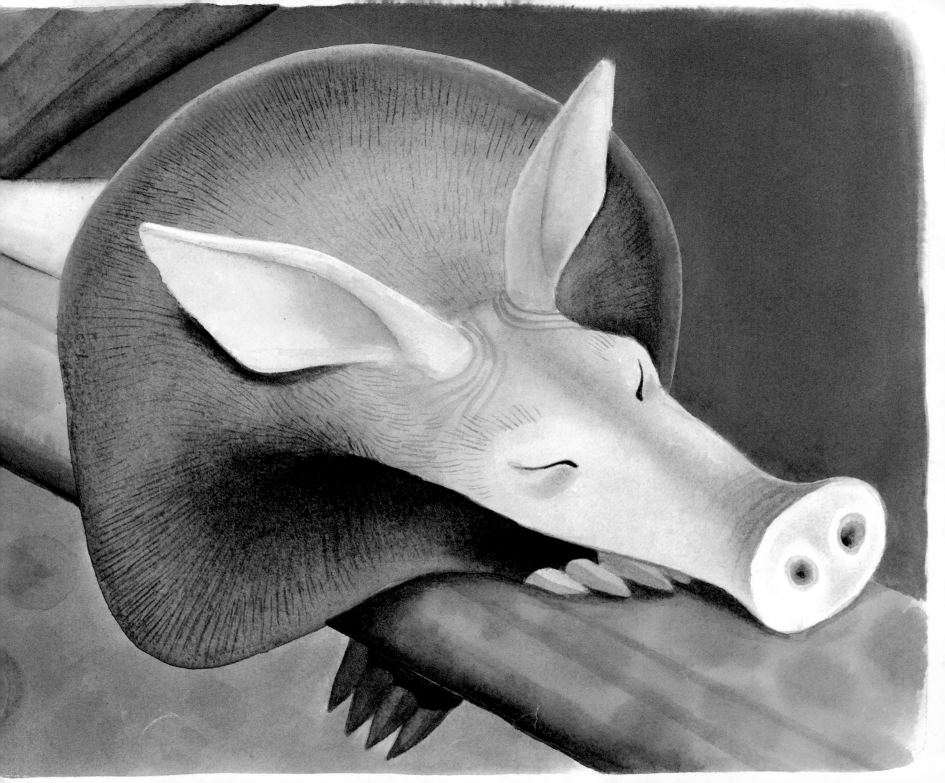

Aardvark only stopped snoring
when the sun came up. Then he
clambered to the ground and
set off to hunt for tasty grubs
and crunchy beetles.

While Aardvark was hunting
for breakfast, Mongoose
had an idea.
  "I will just have to annoy him
more than he annoys me,"
he decided.

First Mongoose had a meeting
with the Monkeys.

Next he went to see Lion.

Then he talked to Rhinoceros.

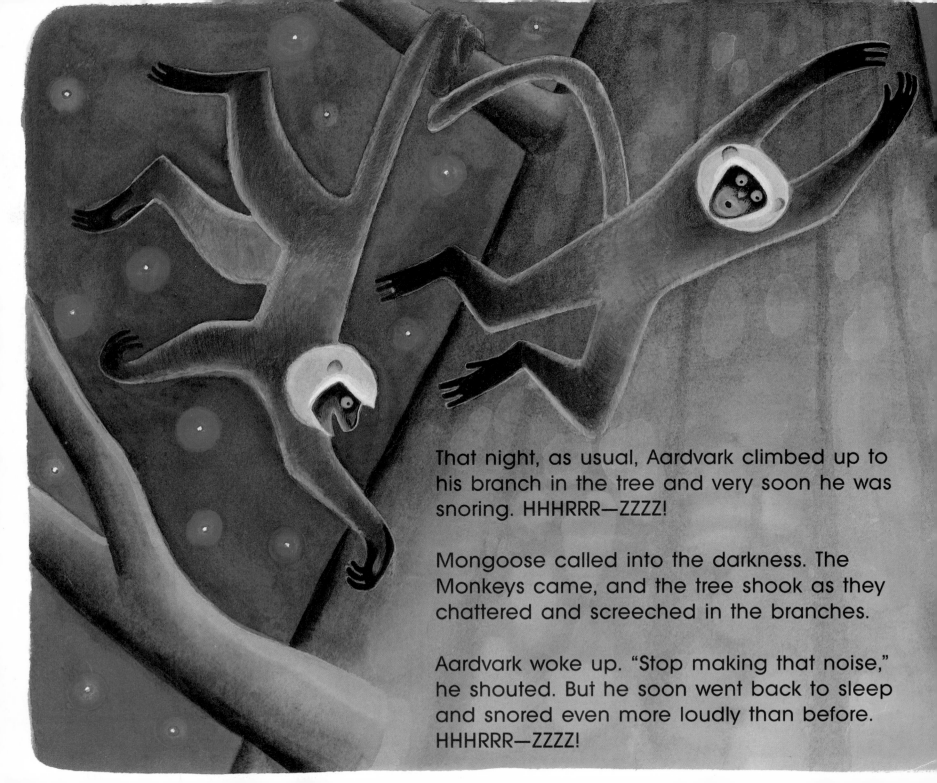

That night, as usual, Aardvark climbed up to his branch in the tree and very soon he was snoring. HHHRRR—ZZZZ!

Mongoose called into the darkness. The Monkeys came, and the tree shook as they chattered and screeched in the branches.

Aardvark woke up. "Stop making that noise," he shouted. But he soon went back to sleep and snored even more loudly than before. HHHRRR—ZZZZ!

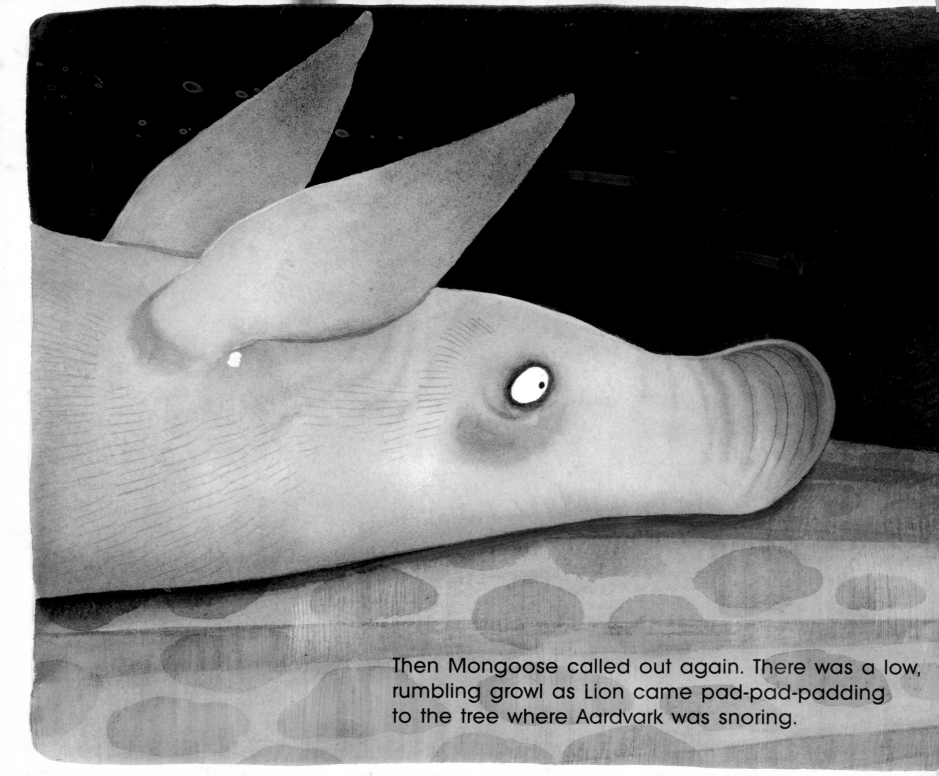

Then Mongoose called out again. There was a low, rumbling growl as Lion came pad-pad-padding to the tree where Aardvark was snoring.

Stretching his legs and reaching high, Lion
SCRAAATCHED the bark with his strong claws.

Aardvark woke up again. "Stop it! Go away!"
he shouted. But soon he was snoring again,
louder than ever. HHHRRR—ZZZZ!

Now Mongoose was very angry. He was so angry that his fur bristled. He sent out another call. The ground trembled as Rhinoceros came puff-puff-puffing to the tree. BUMP! Aardvark nearly fell off the branch when Rhinoceros pushed his fat bottom against the trunk.

"Go away! Leave me alone!" cried Aardvark. But still he did not stay awake for long. HHHRRR—ZZZZ!

"We need help," puffed Rhinoceros. "I'll tell you what we'll do."

Soon there came a munch-munch-munching
sound from the roots of the tree.
Aardvark just kept on snoring.

Suddenly there was a loud snap and a crack.
SNAP! went the roots. CRAAAAACK went the tree
and it toppled over.
Aardvark bounced to the ground.

He picked himself up and glared at the other animals. "Who did that? Who pushed my tree over?" he demanded.

"Not me," said Lion.

"Not me," said Rhinoceros.

"Not us," said the Monkeys.

Aardvark snorted at Mongoose. "It was you."

"Not me," said Mongoose. "They did it." And he pointed at the broken roots.

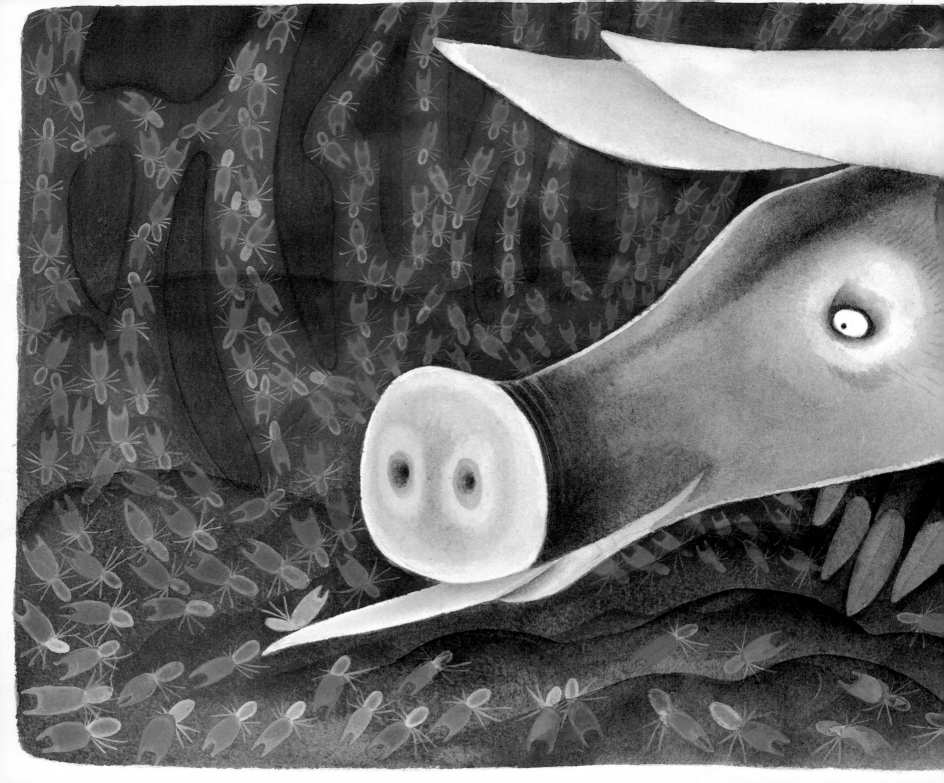

Aardvark saw that the roots of the tree had been eaten away by hundreds of termites.

"I'm going to gobble you up," he threatened. He stuck out his long tongue and ate some of the termites. Yum-yum. He licked his lips. "I think I'll eat you all."

The termites hurried away with Aardvark following and eating as many as he could reach with his tongue.

In the morning the termites hid in
the castles of sand and mud which
they had built to protect themselves.
But at night they still came out to eat the trees.

And from that time to this, Aardvark has slept during the day and eaten termites at night.

And Mongoose and the other animals sleep peacefully because they are no longer disturbed by Aardvark's awful snoring.

PRINTED IN BELGIUM BY
proost
INTERNATIONAL BOOK PRODUCTION